The Little Red Hen

Clarion Books
a Houghton Mifflin Company imprint
215 Park Avenue South, New York, NY 10003
Copyright © 1973 by Paul Galdone
All rights reserved.
For information about permission to reproduce
selections from this book, write to Permissions,
Houghton Mifflin Company,
215 Park Avenue South, New York, NY 10003.
Printed in the USA

Library of Congress Catalog Card Number: 72-97770
ISBN 0-395-28803-7   Paperback ISBN 0-89919-349-8
Book designed by Paul Galdone.

HOR 30 29 28 27 26 25 24 23 22 21

The Little Red Hen

PAUL GALDONE

CLARION BOOKS
NEW YORK

Once upon a time
a cat and a dog and a mouse
and a little red hen
all lived together in a cozy little house.

1.

The cat liked to sleep all day
on the soft couch.

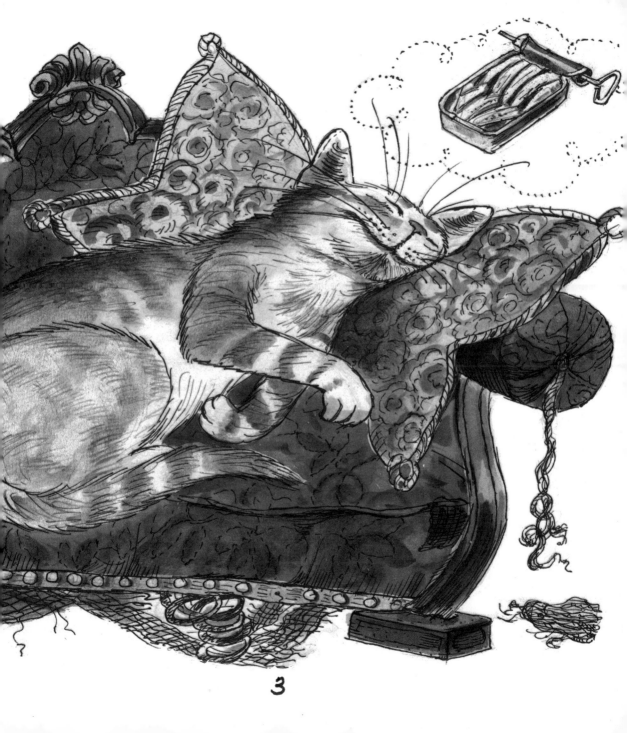

The dog liked to nap all day
on the sunny back porch.

5.

And the mouse liked to snooze all day
in the warm chair by the fireside.

7.

So the little red hen had to do all the housework.

She cooked the meals and washed the dishes
and made the beds. She swept the floor
and washed the windows
and mended the clothes.

She raked the leaves
and mowed the grass
and hoed the garden.

One day when she was hoeing the garden
she found some grains of wheat.

10.

"Who will plant this wheat?" cried the little red hen.

11.

"Not I," said the cat.

"Not I," said the dog.

12.

"Not I," said the mouse.

13.

"Then I will," said the little red hen. And she did.

Each morning the little red hen watered the wheat and pulled the weeds.

Soon the wheat pushed through the ground and began to grow tall.

14

When the wheat was ripe,
the little red hen asked,
"Who will cut this wheat?"

"N⊙t I," said the cat.

"N⊙t I," said the dog.

"N⊙t I," said the mouse.

"Then I will," said the little red hen.
And she did.

17.

When the wheat was all cut, the little red hen asked,
"Now, who will take this wheat to the mill
to be ground into flour?"

"Not I," said the cat.

"Not I," said the dog.

"Not I," said the mouse.

18

"Then I will," said the little red hen. And she did.

19

The little red hen returned from the mill
carrying a small bag of fine white flour.
"Who will make a cake from this fine white flour?"
asked the little red hen.

20

"Not I," said the cat.

"Not I," said the dog.

"Not I," said the mouse.

21.

"Then I will," said the little red hen. And she did.

She gathered sticks and made a fire in the stove.
Then she took milk and sugar and eggs and butter
and mixed them in a big bowl
with the fine white flour.

When the oven was hot she poured
the cake batter into a shining pan
and put it in the oven.

23

Soon a delicious smell
filled the cozy little house.

24

The cat got off the soft couch
and strolled into the kitchen.

25

The dog got up from the sunny back porch
and came into the kitchen.

26

The mouse jumped down from his warm chair
and scampered into the kitchen.

The little red hen
was just taking
a beautiful cake
out of the oven.

"Who will eat this cake?"
asked the little red hen.

"I will!" cried the cat.
"I will!" cried the dog.
"I will!" cried the mouse.

31.

But the little red hen said,

"All by myself
I planted the wheat,
I tended the wheat,
I cut the wheat,
I took the wheat to the mill
to be ground into flour.

All by myself
I gathered the sticks,
I built the fire,
I mixed the cake.
And
all by myself

32

And so she did,
to the very last crumb.

After that,

whenever there was work to be done,
the little red hen had three very eager helpers.